Does God Ever Sleep?

*Goodnight
and
Joan Sauro (S)*

JOAN SAURO, CSJ

Walking Together, Finding the Way

SKYLIGHT PATHS®
PUBLISHING
Woodstock, Vermont

To my mother, Helen
"Goodnight and God bless"

Does God Ever Sleep?

2005 First Printing

Text and photos © 2005 by Joan Sauro

Library of Congress Cataloging-in-Publication Data

Sauro, Joan.

Does God ever sleep? / Joan Sauro.

p. cm.

Summary: In response to a child's questions at bedtime, her loved ones tell her what God does to tuck the world into bed each night, from dimming the lights to sending a breeze that sings a lullaby of leaves through the trees.

ISBN 1-59473-110-1 (pbk.)

[1. Bedtime—Fiction. 2. God—Fiction. 3. Stories in rhyme.] I. Title.

PZ8.3.S2453Do 2005

[E]—dc22

2005009088

10 9 8 7 6 5 4 3 2 1

Manufactured in China
Cover design concept: Michael Ingersoll and Greg Zukowski
Cover design & interior typesetting: Jenny Buono

SkyLight Paths Publishing is creating a place where people of different spiritual traditions come together for challenge and inspiration, a place where we can help each other understand the mystery that lies at the heart of our existence.

SkyLight Paths sees both believers and seekers as a community that increasingly transcends traditional boundaries of religion and denomination—people wanting to learn from each other, walking together, finding the way.

SkyLight Paths, "Walking Together, Finding the Way," and colophon are trademarks of LongHill Partners, Inc., registered in the U.S. Patent and Trademark Office.

Walking Together, Finding the Way
Published by SkyLight Paths Publishing
A Division of LongHill Partners, Inc.
Sunset Farm Offices, Route 4, P.O. Box 237
Woodstock, VT 05091
Tel: (802) 457-4000   Fax: (802) 457-4004
www.skylightpaths.com

Every night when it
came time for bed,
she asked a hundred
quⅇstiⅇns
instead.

"Does everyone sleep?

Do bikes and trees,
birds and balloons?

Does God ever sleep?"

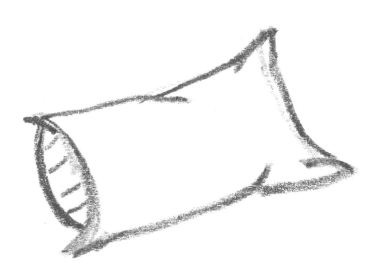

"If you close your eyes
and slip into bed,
we'll tell you a story,"
her loved ones said.

"When the busy day
is almost done,
God lowers the shades
and turns off the sun.

"As night comes near,
        the hills lie down
                without a sigh,
                        without a sound.

"Down by the water
God rolls the stones
to their warm

riverbed homes.

"Then comes a breeze,
God's singing in the trees,
'Hush a bye, hush a bye,'
lullaby of leaves.

"God walks among flowers
                    snug in garden beds.
'Close your bright eyes.
                    Rest your lovely heads.'

"When birds in their nests
  lie down to rest,
    God tucks them in tight
      under covers of night.

"tots on cots

bags in huddles

ladders
and
cans

rain in puddles

cars under blankets of blue."

"Does God sleep, too?"

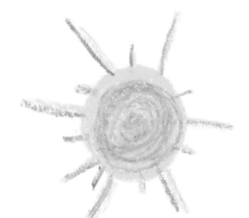

"Day and night

God watches over you.

"Sometimes God rests
on a pillow of cloud,

low in the sky
and always close by.

Zzz z z

"Lie down, now,
and rest your sleepy head
on the pillow of cloud
floating on your bed.

"Rock a bye, rock
             to the land of nod.
Hush a bye, hush,
             dear child of God."